For the Gabrielson girls:
Abbie, who shared her love of pink
with me, and Sara, who danced her
way into my heart. — NG

To lovely little Fée — LM

Groundwood Books / House of Anansi Press
110 Spadina Avenue, Suite 801
Toronto, Ontario M5V 2K4

Distributed in the USA by Publishers Group West
1700 Fourth Street, Berkeley, CA 94710

We acknowledge for their financial support of our
publishing program the Canada Council for the Arts, the
Government of Canada through the Book Publishing
Industry Development Program (BPIDP) and the Ontario
Arts Council.

ONTARIO ARTS COUNCIL
CONSEIL DES ARTS DE L'ONTARIO

Library and Archives Canada Cataloguing in Publication
Gregory, Nan
Pink / by Nan Gregory ; pictures by Luc Melanson.
ISBN-13: 978-0-88899-781-4
ISBN-10: 0-88899-781-7
I. Melanson, Luc II. Title.
PS8563.R4438P55 2007   jC813'.54   C2006-906682-5

The illustrations were done digitally.
Design by Michael Solomon
Printed and bound in China

PINK

Nan Gregory

pictures by Luc Melanson

GROUNDWOOD BOOKS | HOUSE OF ANANSI PRESS | TORONTO BERKELEY

Vivi is dizzy with wanting pink. The kind Merrillee and Miranda and Janine have. "The Pinks," Vivi calls them, but not out loud. Every day at school they parade their glory — from hair bows to tippy toes, every shade of perfect pink.

Vivi lives in a big brown building. Her mom cleans the halls to make ends meet. Her dad drives a truck to faraway places.

Vivi imagines where the Pinks live — in houses, pink inside like shells, their dads home every night.

"The Pinks have all the pink," she tells her mom.

"There's plenty of pink for everyone," says Mom.

"Not perfect pink," says Vivi. But baby Gabriel is hungry now and Mom can't hear.

"The Pinks have all the perfect pink," she tells her dad.

"Nope," he says, and blows a little lick on his harmonica. "You've got some in your cheeks."

Don't they want to understand? Vivi is wild with wanting.

One dead of winter afternoon, running an
errand for her mom, Vivi finds a wonder the
Pinks don't have. It stands in the window of
My Little Darling, Gifts for the Fortunate Child,
all lit up like crystal — a dainty bride doll in a
dress of glistening pink petals, layers and
layers, each one glazed with rainbow light.

Vivi feasts her eyes until the storekeeper
bustles out, bundled up for going home.

"You like my doll," she says.

"She's perfect pink."

"Look all you like." The storekeeper's voice
is warm and sweet as the lock clicks shut.

The next day Vivi is back. "Hello, hello," tinkles a merry bell as she marches in.

"What's this?" the storekeeper asks.

"It's for the doll in the window."

The storekeeper laughs and laughs. "Keep your money," she says, and pushes the piggy bank into Vivi's arms.

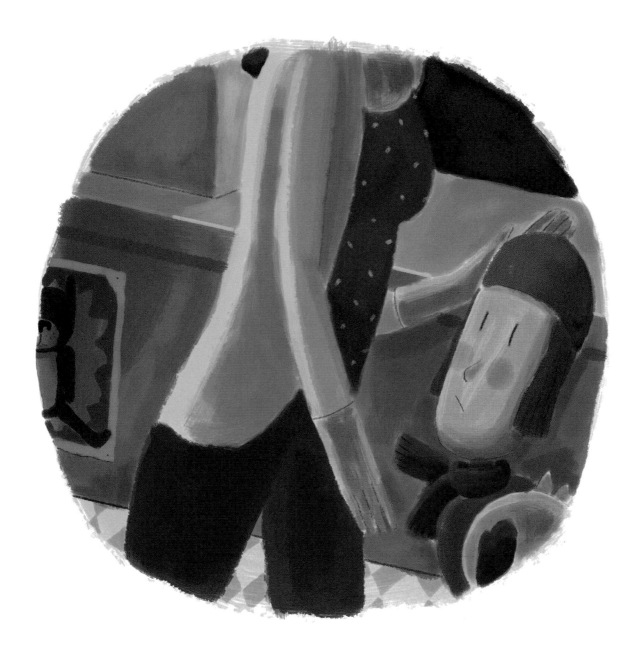

She leads Vivi toward the window. Will she say, "You love her so much, she belongs with you?" Vivi's heart is breaking up into stars.

"You'll have to save and save if you want this doll," says the warm honey voice. The merry bell jingles. The storekeeper's hand presses Vivi out onto the sidewalk. Vivi's breath is white in the icy air.

At dinner Vivi makes an announcement. "I'm going to save and save," she says. "I'm going to buy a pink bride doll."

"You could do errands for the neighbors," says Dad.

"Put a notice in the laundry room," says Mom.

The notice reads:

Vivi walks the next-door dog. The man in the basement gives her some bottles to cash in. A woman upstairs needs help with her shopping. Nickels and dimes clank to the bottom of Vivi's bank.

At recess the words blurt out of her.

"I have a pink doll. Her dress is like a sugar flower." Vivi's fingers make petals in the air.

The Pinks circle her close. "If you really have a doll," Janine taunts, "why don't you bring her to school?"

Vivi defends herself. "She's still in the store, but I'm getting her."

"What store?" Merrillee wants to know.

"My Little Darling."

The Pinks whirl away.

Ice melts. Days turn to spring. Vivi's bank is filling slowly. One Saturday at breakfast her mom says, "Let's all have a pink day today."

"Isn't pink for girls?" Dad asks.

"Pink is for everyone," says Mom. "We'll have a picnic. We'll make a list of every pink thing we see."

"I've got to fix my truck," Dad says.

Mom makes white bread sandwiches with raspberry jam. Then she makes cranberry tea. It shines like a ruby as it pours into the thermos.

"I thought we might stop at the bakery for a treat," Mom says. Vivi thinks yes to that. She helps snug Gabriel into his jacket.

Dad is under the truck.

"Coming?" Mom asks. He catches them up at the corner.

"Look at this," he says.

"It's like a pink room up here," Vivi calls.

At the bakery they each choose a little cake with pink icing. Vivi's has a rose on top. At the pet store they admire the ears on the baby mice. Mom takes out a notebook and writes down: cherry blossoms, petits fours, baby mice ears.

The park is all decked out in pink. They spread Vivi's old baby blanket under a plum tree. It's a lake of petals underneath.

They watch five wedding parties taking pictures. Mom writes down: pink flowers, baby blanket, flower-girl finery.

Vivi wipes her fingers on the grass and sips ruby tea from the lid of the thermos. Dad lies with his head in Mom's lap. Gabriel dozes in his carriage.

"I love picnics," says Mom.

"Pinknics," Vivi says into her ear. "Because everything is pink."

Then it's quiet for a bit, and out of the quiet Dad says, "One night on a long haul across the prairies, I saw a wonderful thing. A truck and trailer driving through the dark, all decked out with lights. Lights all over the cab, all down the sides of the load."

"Were they pink?" Vivi asks.

"All colors. At first I didn't know what it was, all lit up like fairyland. Ever since, I've wanted lights like that for my truck."

"Why don't you get them?"

Her dad laughs. "You can't have everything. Lights like that cost a bundle."

Vivi jumps up. "Do you want to see my bride doll? She costs a bundle, too. She's on the way home. We could add her to our list. Please?"

The bride doll is gone from the window.

"The storekeeper probably moved her inside," Vivi says. "I'll go check." The handle rushes out of her grasp with a ring-ting-ting of the merry bell.

Merrillee sweeps out. She has the doll. She is saying, "Oh, thank you, Auntie Anne. This is the perfect present."

The pink crystal petal skirt flounces past Vivi's face. Auntie Anne follows. Vivi, her mom and her dad stand like sillies in the air of her perfume.

Mom laughs, high and helpless. Dad reaches out to take Vivi in his arms. She elbows him away. She is not a baby to be comforted with hugs. He turns on his heel and strides off home. Mom hurries after. Rickety-rick, the wheels on the carriage wobble keeping up.

"Come along, Vivi," Mom calls.

It's hard to go fast when your heart is a stone.

When Vivi gets home, her dad is sitting alone on the steps, hunched over his harmonica. His breath wheezes in and out. His big boots thump the beat. Vivi listens for a bit and the music wraps around her. Her heels rise up. She begins to dance.

Up go her hands as the notes swoop up
Down twists her body as the tune threads down
Her feet skip hop for a cup of ruby tea
Her legs jump high for the blossoms on the trees
Up and down, up and down.
The notes bend her knees and she craves pink pearls
The sound comes puffing and she waves to the doll
Her fingers flutter out, feeling the tone
She races in a circle just for fun
Round and round, round and round.
The tune is blue, it reels her in
She steps and shimmies and croons a hum
She swings up high on a lilt of sound
She whirls down dizzy on the spinning ground
Up and down, round and round
Round and round, and that's the end.

Vivi flops down beside her dad to catch her breath. He knocks the spit out of his harmonica and gives her a little grin. She leans against him and watches the neighborhood rock back to level.

"I'm sorry you can't get lights for your truck," she says.

"Don't be sorry," he says. "Wanting things makes good music." He sneaks an arm around her shoulders. "Good dancing, too."

Behind the trees the clouds blush perfect pink.
Vivi nestles close.

Her dad said you can't have everything. But just for a moment, Vivi knows she does.